# Operation Sabotage

## A StarSoldier Chronicle

### C.R. Coyne

# Feedback

Please leave honest feedback.
Your opinion is important to me!

# Table of Contents

# Also By CR Coyne

Nothing ever happens on Oz, that's why the Skipper had chosen this lonely non-technology spot to retire.  But no matter where you go in the universe your past catches up with you.  And for Yaz, the squad, and the Skipper the past will cost more than they can bear.

Buy your copy today!

# Also By CR Coyne

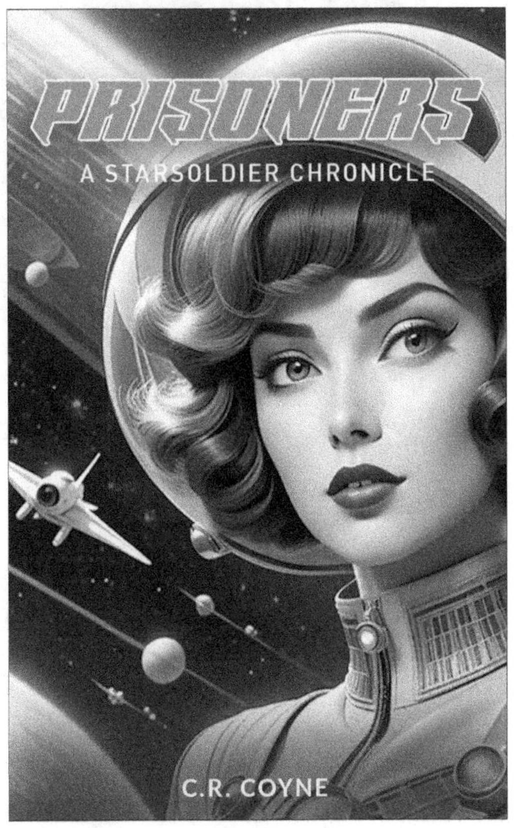


Regulus V was a colony of eight billion humans, rich and comfortable in their adopted home.  Great place to visit.  But when the entire system becomes a wasteland the StarSoldiers must face an ancient evil as old as the stars themselves and stop it before more die!

Buy your copy today!

# Also By CR Coyne

The colony of Altair IV seems peaceful enough, well at least from space.  But when the squad lands they find a dead colony and creatures that can't possibly exist!

Buy your copy today!

# Also By CR Coyne

Fastbuck is one of the worst places in the human sphere and everyone knows it. So it's kind of hard to get excited about saving the place.  But the Star Soldiers don't play favorites.  But when the doom of Fastbuck decides it has other ideas than mere destruction the squad suddenly has more than one planet to worry about!

Buy your copy today!

# Galactic Area of Human Sphere

# Star Map of Notable Sites

# History of the Mohawk Tribe

The Mohawk are traditionally the keepers of the Eastern Door of the Iroquois Confederacy, also known as the Six Nations Confederacy or the Haudenosaunee Confederacy. Our original homeland is the north eastern region of New York State extending into southern Canada and Vermont. Prior to contact with Europeans the Mohawk settlements populated the Mohawk Valley of New York State. Through the centuries Mohawk influence extended far beyond their territory and was felt by the Dutch who settled on the Hudson River and in Manhattan. The Mohawks' location as the Iroquois nation closest to Albany and Montreal, and the fur traders there, gave them considerable influence among the other Tribes. This location has also contributed directly to a long and beautifully complicated history.

In the 1750s, to relieve crowding at Kahnawake and to move closer to the Iroquois homeland, the French Jesuits established a mission at the present site on the St. Regis River. The Mohawk people had continually used this site at the confluence of the St. Lawrence River Valley as part of our fishing and hunting grounds prior to the building of the first church. "Akwesasne" as it is known today, translates roughly to "Land where the partridge drums" has always been a prime location due to the confluence of several small rivers and the St. Lawrence River.

# Operation Sabotage

*A StarSoldier Chronicles Story*

*Raven Coyne*

*"I raise my flag; dye my clothes.  It's a revolution I suppose."—Imagine Dragons.*

"If anything it looks more like a gas giant than a terrestrial planet," I say as I'm looking at the sensor data.  Sergeant Murphy grunts his agreement then flips a few switches and gets a few more details.

"The coordinates are right Yaz."  He says trying to puzzle out what I've been trying to figure out for three days.

"Yeah, but the planet is," I stop and stumble over my words, "wrong.  Look at it, if that is an E-Class world I'll eat my emergency rations."  E-rations are notoriously awful you see.

"Can we land on it?  Even in survival gear." Sarge asks me as he keeps checking the star charts.

"I don't know, the sensors can't make heads nor tails of the readings we're getting.  I wouldn't want to gamble on it being nothing but gas.  Are you sure we are in the right place?"  I shouldn't bother to ask of course, it's the right place.  I think.

"According HARVE this is the place.  Star fixes are right, mean distance to the primary is correct.  Hell, even the asteroids are right.  Is anything right in your readings?"

I bend over the scanner and try and make sense out of the mass of contradictions I am looking at "it's the right size for Topaz, that's about it.  I keep getting an odd radiation reading, probably gravity anomalies."

Sarge straightens up folds his arms over his chest and starts to assemble what we know and don't in his head.  This is the part of his job that makes me never want that extra stripe.  "We land, start the revival cycle on everyone.  Once Dutch is up and perking have her prep the armored lander."

I salute and trot off to the med-pit and start the revival cycle for everyone.  I watch the vitals.  As I watch I notice that Striker has a fever not too high just enough.  Checking everyone else they all seem in good health.  I'll leave Striker in the tube and alert HARVE to start treatment.  I wait for everyone else to get up. Dutch is first she stretches that fantastic body of hers, generous chest, legs that most women would kill for with arms the size of tree trunks.  She smiles at me "are ve there? Vhen do ve fly?" I in turn have to smile at that. There is only one thing that makes Dutch tick, flying.

I lick my lips and say "yeah, we're sorta there. Sarge wants you to prep the armored lander. Tut sweet."

Dutch frowns at my answer, "that's tut de suite."

I roll my eyes as Miss I-speak-five-languages instructs me, saying only "yeah prep the armored lander," using my I'm the corporal and you're not voice. She shrugs and heads off. Yeldon gets up picks up her dirty socks off the bay floor and wanders out without a word. Odd she's more of a morning person than that. Oh well, I head back to the bridge to find Murphy still staring at readouts.

He turns to me and while pulling his lip out with thumb and forefinger says, "anything unusual happen when I was hibernating?"

"We passed through a solar flare, it was hot but well within the tolerances of the ship's coolers. Other than that not especially, no. I helped HARVE fly in he and I checked out the planet. HARVE and I came to the same conclusion this ain't the right place. I gave it three days of real research then woke you up. By the way, Striker is running a fever

I'm leaving him in and letting the auto-doc take care of it."

Sergeant Murphy nods at that flips a telltale on the control board then says "how bad?"

"One point above normal, he's probably fighting off that Tellurian Whiskey he bought."

"Keep an eye on him, he has the same genetic enhancements as everyone else on this ship, a fever falls outside his body's immune programming."

"Genetherapy is all well and good but it can't cope with what it's never encountered.  I doubt the docs back home ever thought of Tellurian Whiskey."

I give a smile and Murph smiles back then flips a switch to the all-call, "listen up rifleman, I want you prepped in four hours ready for inspection.  We're down one soldier so everyone is going to have to pick up the slack.  Currently, we are in orbit around Planet Topaz.  Our mission is simple, pull out a cultural assessment team so they can report to United Earth on the conditions here.  As you are aware Topaz is a retrograde colony.  They seem to be making progress back to industrialization, that means hands off the natives.  This is all covert we find the team and pull out nice and quiet. That is all."

"How do you lose the ability to manufacture?" I ask idly.

Sarge shrugs "according to the last survey these folks are just past throwing rocks at each other. Something went wrong down there. Anyway not our problem. Get preped."

"One last, it still looks like the wrong planet," I say.

Murphy shoots me a cold look then shrugs, again, and says "we'll just have to deal with that when we get down there."

"Who stays behind?" I ask.

"No one, we all land," Murphy says and turns to go.

That's not like Sergeant-by-the-book Murphy at all. "Sir, I'm the last to pull regs you know that. But the regulation says someone stays up here."

Murphy turns to me a tired sigh escapes his lips, "with Striker down, I want as many eyes as possible dirt-side. We get in and then get back out."

"Yes sir," I say. I've made my point no need to stretch this into a punishment detail for myself.

I make it to the landing deck with five minutes to spare. I tug at my native garb and keep playing with the pant holster and pistol therein. I wait for everyone else, Murphy comes in, he's dressed like a Renaissance Festival barkeep. He looks around and then waits for the other two. Dutch wanders in snaps to attention salutes; she looks great in the period peasant dress she's wearing. She climbs into the cockpit of the armored lander and starts flipping switches and setting dials. The ugly brute is the only craft we have that has a wrap on it. The paint job on the thing can blend into the surroundings and you never see it. It's not invisible mind you, just camouflaged. Yeldon is late, I'm about to go roust her out of her quarters when she comes in salutes, and starts to board the lander. Sarge clears his throat and says with what I think admirable calm, "you're naked rifleman."

It's true, Yeldon is buck except for the webbing she's wearing and a pair of dress parade gloves with her Type-10 slung over her shoulder. Her forage cap is tipped at a jaunty angle and at first, I can't quite figure out what's wrong with it. Upon closer inspection of the hat, and nothing else mind you, I see she has a daisy sticking out of the brim. "Yes sir!" Yeldon retorts brightly, "who needs clothes when there's Andies to kill?"

Sarge nods, "true enough rifleman. Good thinking." Sarge starts to load up as my jaw hits the deck, bounces back to my face then does it again for emphasis.

"Sergeant!" I snap maybe a bit too loud, "Rifleman Yeldon cannot complete the mission while staying covertly dressed, or in this case undressed like that. These folks do have clothes, I'm pretty sure a naked woman toting a Type-10 will attract attention."

"You're right corporal. Rifleman go get dressed."

Yeldon frowns and looks crestfallen, "Do I have to?"

"Okay that's it, I'm pulling regs. Sergeant, I am assuming command of this ship and crew. Rifleman Yeldon and Sergeant Murphy report to Medical." They both start toward the door and I add, "Rifleman Yeldon put something on." Both look me over shrug at the same time and head out of the launch bay. I look up at Dutch who is still adjusting her cockpit controls. "Dutch I don't think we're going anywhere for a while."

She nods giggles and starts to climb out. "You don't think a naked rifleman can pull off this mission?" With a heavy laugh, she walks out.

# III

Chandler flies through the door and pulls it tight. Mary looks at him worriedly and asks "did anyone see you?"

Peering back outside Chandler shakes his head, "no they're still combing the other side of the village.  We have got to get out."  Mary nods and shows the already packed backpack.  "do you have the recorder, scanner suite, and most of all the radio?"

"Everything.  Now let's go before they find us!  I don't want to end up like Childers."  Mary says that sends a chill down Chandler's spine, he can still hear the screaming.  The two slink out of the small rude hut and start to disappear into the deep woods beyond the house while the glow of torches rushing this way and that from the mob lights their path somewhat.  Stopping where they know they can't be seen they watch the crowd stop at the small hut and light fire to it while chanting in unison.  Mary rolls her eyes "religion at work."

Chandler takes her arm carefully and guides her deeper into the woods saying simply "yeah."  For twenty minutes they just keep running, stumbling, getting hit in the face with branches, but walking some more.  Deeper into the old growth woods they go letting its dark mystery consume them and hopefully save them.  Mary after a while breaks the silence with "where the blue blazes are those StarSoldiers?  They're two days late!"

Chandler nods his agreement with the sentiment, "who knows?  Maybe got lost along the way.  When we get to the caves break out the radio and give it a try.  Maybe this time we get lucky."

Mary nods, "who knows?  We have to get lucky sooner or later."

# IV

The auto-doc starts a full examination of both Yeldon and Murphy.  Murphy seems more in line with his usual self than Yeldon, well only just.

Yeldon's a free spirit true, not this free mind you.  The auto-doc readouts show a slight temperature in both.  Just like Striker which makes me wonder what would happen if I let him get up?  I decide to have myself checked to my relief I'm normal.  Or as normal as I get.  HARVE interprets the readouts for me saying, "same symptoms as Striker.  I'm anathematized if I know what it is."  After that, I seal myself in a side room of the med-pit and ask "HARVE how about we just put those two into tubes?  Maybe head home."

"Not the best idea you've had Yaz," HARVE says, "first off Striker's temp is getting worse, so storing our sick won't stop the infection.  Two I need those two awake to run more tests on them."  I nod reluctantly.  HARVE then says, "we're getting a transmission from the surface, it's weak but readable."

I press the com-control on the desk in the room, "this is U.E.S. Mohawk who am I speaking with?"

"Oh GAWDS!  Chandler they're answering."  The voice is desperate and comes through the speaker in a hiss, "this is Doctor Dayner of survey team twelve.  How soon for pickup?  We have a code red, I repeat to you a code red."

I frown and HARVE mumbles to me "never rains but it pours."  I drop my head to my chest.  Can it get any worse?   "State the nature of your emergency please."

"We have been discovered by the natives.  They are searching for us.  We are to be killed as witches."

My eyes roll up to HARVE'S screen and mouth silently "witches?  Really?"  HARVE stays impassive.  He's never surprised by human behavior.  I press the intercom button and sit down, "Dutch, heat up the armored lander."

"She ist cold as a mackerel.  It vill take me ten hours to prep her again.  I shut everything down thinking we wouldn't need her until tomorrow."

"Great, thraggeling great."  I punch savagely at the radio button one more time clear my throat and say calmly, "we will attempt a pickup in ten hours Doctor.  Can you hold out that long?"

"We've taken shelter in a cave several miles from the village.  They'll find us eventually.  But we'll do our best."

"I promise doc we're coming as fast as we can." I switch to Dutch and say simply "speed it up Dutch we've got people's lives at stake now."

"Dutch out."

"I hate to add to your problems," HARVE starts out meekly.

I nod and say quietly "go ahead, add."

"What about our people?  And how do you intend on saving those people with just you?"

# V

The Witch Hunter looks over the small now burned out hut carefully pulling on his beard, "and you say they lived here?"

"Yes Lord Taylon.  Tom over there observed them speaking into a small box which spoke back in a queer tone.  He reported it to me immediately. We tried to arrest the witches for you but one was killed by accident."

"You mean torn apart by an angry mob," The Witch Hunter says in sarcasm.  The Mayor's head goes down in shame, "never mind.  Organize your militia I shall use them to conduct a search.  The witches must be found.  Ten were identified last year in Timber.  The old hate has come back to us. This time we are prepared."  The man then looks over the wreck and finds a small black ovoid box among the ash.  Picking it up he flips open the top. The small device winks and purrs in a steady hum. Saying an invoking protection prayer he closes the lid and pockets the odd device.

The Mayor watching all this shudders, "what hellspawn is that?"  He shoves a frightened finger at the hunter's pocket.

"Nothing we cannot handle Citizen of Truth. Now go about your business.  Get me my militia." Taylon then circles the house and summons his two trusty guards who stand at attention and salute. "You understand your mission?"  The two hard-faced men nod they're understanding and dog trot into the dark woods.  Taylon strokes his well kept beard pulls the small box back out and looks over the device again.  Muttering "damn," quietly he puts the device back in his pocket.  He walks to the center of town to size up the motley collection of drunks, farmers, whores, and general rabble that line up for inspection.  Shaking his head he says to all "you're not the Primacies Guard that's for sure, but you'll have to do.  You understand the threat. Witches have been living among you for some time. I expect full cooperation and obedience from each and every one of you, as you allowed the witches to at first live here unmolested and then lost them you are under interdiction unless I remove it.  I will do so only if you obey and aid my noble cause, which is yours as well."  The rabble shuffle their feet and mumble their accent.  Turning to the dark woods ahead Lord Taylon says "in there our quarry lies. Forward!"

One young man points a shaking finger "but Lord, that's where they consort with demons."

"You have nothing to fear Citizen of Truth, I am with you.  The righteous shall prevail."  And with that, the small well dressed man his red robes of office trailing behind him marches into the woods.  His courage convinces the others to follow.  That and the threat of Interdiction for the village for its blasphemy."

# VI

I decide watching Yeldon and my boss playing jacks is not solving any problems and I walk out of the med-pit.  The idea that all my ideas, hair-brained or not have now become orders is frightening.  We have just six hours left to try and find a cure for the ailment aboard and save our people below.  I enter the bridge to find Dutch playing with some controls and checking readouts, "please tell me you're not in the mood for jacks."

Dutch looks over her shoulder and ruffles up her forehead in confusion, "vas ist jacks?"

I sigh "how close are we to ready?  And did you get checked out by the auto-doc?"

"Three more hours, I cut the time as best I could.  And yes sir I did, temp normal.  Everything normal."

I nod distracted by the image of the planet.  This place looks totally wrong.  There is just no other way to say it.  "Dutch is the penance ready as well as the lander"

"Yes sir, I warmed it and the shuttle as well.  You know just in case."  Dutch answers.

"I want you to fly me in the penance."

"Ve will be seen, Corporal."

"I don't want to land, I just want an up close view of the planet.  Let's get going."  I know we can take the penance it's designed to be up and running in minutes instead of hours of prep work.  It's not entirely the safest vehicle we have but it does the trick and gets you home.  Most of the time.  Dutch and I enter the landing bay and take off in the little craft that scoots us toward the planet.  "The closer we come the less it looks like Topaz," Dutch says and I have to agree.  We orbit once then she sets us on a gentle glide path.  As we enter the troposphere Dutch grunts in an alarming way, "I'm losing instrumentation!  Hang on this is going to get rougher before it gets better."  The penance plummets toward the planet and Dutch tries to dive and roll to gain control.  But it doesn't work.  I look over and all the control boards are dark, Dutch is literally flying blind.

"What can I do?"  I ask.

"Shut up," Dutch offers and I nod and shut up. The Penance must lose a hundred thousand feet in minutes and we spin and spin.  I've forgotten which way the stars are at this point, but Dutch holds tight and keeps flying.  "I'm starting the landing run!"

"Landing run?   We can't land, covert remember?"

"It's that or die, vhich do you vant?"

"Land Dracula!  Land!"  I shout as the ground rushes up to greet us.  The small ship slides into a sandy beach by a good sized lake.  I just close my eyes and hope my death won't hurt too much, the craft leaps back into the air and then settles halfway into the water and stops.  I open my eyes and look around at my new home.  "Terrific.  Thank you Pilot, I still have all my limbs.  My pants are filled but other than that I am fine."

Dutch giggles and slaps the control board. "Something in the atmosphere did this."

"What, you're saying something in the atmosphere cut the controls and engines?"

"This craft had one hundred percent capability until ve hit the air.  That I am sure of Corporal." Dutch asserts and I never argue with a pilot that just saved my life.  They may decide not to next time.  And there is always a next time.

Then a blinding thought hits my mind.  I snap my fingers and look at Dutch.  "Did you take the genetherapy upgrade before we left Jupiter Station?"

Dutch licks her lips, "ah, vell there vas a lot to do before ve left and I..."

"I didn't take it either.  But everyone else on board did Dutch..." I start putting ideas to deductions when I hear a loud bang on the side of the Penance.

"Velkomen committee." Dutch says and looking out I see what she means, about twenty angry natives start closing in on us using spears and bows and arrows.  Dutch grabs up her Type-10 but I put a hand on her.

"Fire the flares," I say.

"Vaz," she says, then gestures to the dead control boards.

Another clunk hits the penance and her face goes red, "alright!"  She pops the canopy aims her rifle at the closest native and presses the trigger.  I wait for the whir and the exploding body but nothing happens.  Dutch looks at the rifle, "Vaz, I think we're in trouble."

"Not as long as our legs work!"  I say and haul her out of the craft and onto the beach.  We make a break for it running madly toward a thick stand of pseudo pinetrees.  The air is like being in the middle of a forest fire, it swirls and dances in our wake.  "Geez if the whole planet is like this!"  I think but suddenly I feel a wet sticky mass fall over me and looking at Dutch see another net fall on her.  We both fall to the ground.  At this point, some big bruiser smashes me in the face and the lights go out.

When I wake back up I am staring at a ceiling made of rough hewn logs and some kind of thatch or native grass.  I look around and don't find Dutch. I sit there for about half an hour alone in the dark until a door opens and there stands a man dressed like what I imagine Cardinal Richelieu looks like in the Three Musketeers.  Right down to the floppy hat, red cassock, and so help me a sword!  I start to giggle which awards me a swift kick in the face by the man.  "Now do you think I am funny?"

"Hilarious," I reply and spit the blood out of my mouth.  Then I get another one for good measure. This one really hurts and I grunt and cry out a bit.

Then he lights a candle and sits on a bare wooden chair.  "That's what I was looking for.  Now corporal we need to talk."

If I was a cat my ears would be swiveling to the front of my head right now eyes big.  "How do you know who I am D'Artagnan?"

"My name is Mark Ellis of United Earth Intelligence, you are a StarSoldier correct?"

"Yeah I am, or what's left of me is. Where is my Pilot?"

"She's safe I have her locked up in my private dwelling," Mr. Earth Intelligence says.

A surge of anger flashes in me, "I see, the girl is safe and the handsome Corporal gets a face full of your horse's poop twice. You have an interesting sense of morals."

Mark Ellis or Cardinal Richelieu or whoever this dude wants to be called passes that by and asks "please hear me out, this colony about forty years ago lost all technology. No one knows why. I was sent here to find out why. During my investigation, I watched the rise of a reactionary named Dadus come to power. He claims that all the past is a lie, an illusion. Anyone who disagrees dies. I've managed to make myself useful to Dadus which has helped my investigation. Now, are you the only StarSoldiers dirt side?"

"Tell you what I answer questions after A: I get to see Dutch making sure she's okay and B: you untie me and stop kicking my face." He sighs nods stands up kicks me one more time again in the kisser and then goes back and unties my hands. I stand up spit more blood out of my mouth and with a bloody but unbowed grin I smash the man's nose. No punch I've ever landed has felt better.

"Okay let's call it even for now, I'll take you to your pilot and try to explain this mess," wiping his nose he takes me out and I see a crowd surrounding the door fear and hate radiating from every single face. I keep quiet the man without a word to the mob takes me to a nice two room piece hovel which is his home while on assignment in this berg.

I whisper under my breath "got it, you needed them to hear me getting the works?"

"You catch on Corporal, slowly but at least you do catch on. We didn't expect pick up for another six months why are you here?"

"We were supposed to pick up a cultural survey team," I answer.

"Then you're who those two were talking to when they got caught by the good citizens of this village. The Mayor reported to Dadus only last night. I managed to get myself assigned here thinking it was something like this." That fills in a few blanks for me at least. Mark Ellis leads me into the hut and there sits Dutch eating some native fruit. Her face is bruised and her wrists are still tied but left in front of her. She looks up concern on her face she comes over with a small cloth and blots the blood off my visage. "Now I don't have a lot of time to explain everything to you two but in brief up to a few years ago this was a thriving colony, something knocked all advanced machinery offline and now these people are left as you see them. Spacecraft can't enter the atmosphere and most high tech ceases to work after a short while."

"How do you lose the ability to manufacture?" I answer my earlier question all at once "all the machines stop. How did you land?"

"I was dropped in a re-entry capsule. Now I need to get you two back to your ship and fast. I am going to tell the Mayor I am taking you with me back to Timber. There for torture and questioning. Stay right here until I come back."

"How about I smash your face again and we escape so we don't get the torture and questioning?" I pipe up.

"Vaz, listen to him. He understands the situation we do not." Dutch admonishes me.

"You didn't get the horse poop treatment," is all I can come back with. I look at Dutch and relent, "fine we'll be right here like good little chitlings." The man leaves and I sit down and wonder if the mission can get any weirder.

"You were trying to tell me something earlier," Dutch asks as I undo the bindings on her wrists. "What was it?"

"Just this whatever is infecting our crew is not a bacteria or virus, it's attacking the mechanical aspects of our bodies.  All of us are given genetherapy right?"  Dutch nods intent on what I am saying "well part of that therapy is nano-robotcs.  To repair damaged cells.  That's what's got everyone acting strangely."  I break off as soon as Mark Ellis returns with two big bruisers by his side dressed like him.  Looking at them both I grin and say quietly "hey Mouse how's tricks?"  The larger of the two men gives me a huge toothy grin his ebony skin making the white perfect teeth stand out.

"I take it you two know each other," Ellis says in passing as he starts to pack.

"Yeah, we went to basic together," Mouse says.

We all pile out of the hut and Dutch and I are placed into a small caged cart, inside the cage note, and driven out of the village.  We ride for several hours until the sun begins to rise.  Only then do I realize how far off the road we are and why the trip has been so crummy.  Finally, we stop in a small sheltered glen in the middle of nowhere.  Ellis jumps down unlocks the cage and helps Dutch out leaving me to fend for myself.  In these situations be a pretty girl, not a pretty boy.  He guides us to a small fold of trees it's only after we get practically nose to nose with the trees I realize there are no trees here.  Just a chemical fuel rocket.  I do a double take, clap my hands, and giggle like a schoolgirl at the thought of a rocket.  Hey, I'm allowed after getting kicked three times in the face. Mouse laughs at me and Mark Ellis nods, "Chemical reactions are unaffected by the phenomena.  This was our ride out of here but you have got to get to your ship and further report back to Earth."  Ellis hands me a small leather-bound book.  "This is my full report.  Please get it to United Earth Intelligence."

I grasp the book "I don't want to take your only way off this dust ball," I start out but Ellis shakes his hand and pats my hand.

"You can fly this thing can't you?"  Mouse asks me.

I smile and jam a thumb at Dutch, "she can, she can fly anything."  Mouse nods and Dutch gives me a you've-got-to-be-kidding-me look.  I grip her shoulder, "you can fly it.  It can only go one direction, up."

# VII

We climb in and Dutch runs over the controls, Ellis and his Starsoldiers get clear, and Dutch hits the activator and the engines of the thing roar into life.  In seconds we are glued to our seats by g-force as the rocket launches into the sky and sends us hurtling above the clouds.  The ride is brutal, but in two minutes we are in space.  In thirty minutes Dutch has maneuvered us to the launch bay of the Mohawk.  With an ever-steady hand, she guides us onto the landing pad settling us down without so much as a bump.  Dutch smiles broadly and says "I haven't had so much fun since Trianglulea."

My head snaps as another revelation is offered for the day "you fought at Triangulea?  Against the Andi fleet?"  Dutch nods and smiles shyly.  I watch as she smiles pats the control board and opens the hatch.

We are greeted by HARVE as he booms out "Hi! How are you Yaz, Dutch?  Guess what?"

"Just tell us please HARVE," I ask too tired and sore to care at this point.

"Nope, you have to guess or I won't tell."  I stop in midstride and my head sinks onto my chest, again. Instead of guessing I manually open the door and march from the launching bay to the bridge Dutch right on my heels. I have to hand crack open the emergency hatch as HARVE has shut down every autodoor to the bridge level. I get to the command station flip open a small covered button and press it in a series of short and long presses. The code disengages HARVE from the control of the ship.

"My hands Yaz! Someone has cut off my hands!" HARVE screams at me.

"You're a computer HARVE you don't have hands." With that, I summon Dutch to do her magic. Taking the pilot swivel she moves the ship out of close orbit around Topaz and sends us out around the small satellite of the planet known as Pyrite.

"Ve should be high enough for no more effects from the planet."

I nod and in a gesture reminiscent of my boss I start to pull at my lower lip, must come with the job. "Dutch we are going hang up here for a bit and hope we correct the problems with computer, ship, and crew. Who knows, maybe it'll just wear off." I snort then shake my head. "Like I can get that lucky."

I look back at Dutch who sits stock still and glued to the screen showing our orbit.  "Vaz, the effect will wear off."  She says so certain that it makes me stop whining and let her roam with her idea.  "When we fought at Triangulea the Andi's had something new, a weapon that shut down all tech in a varship.  It vas no good, the power consumption was enormous and it only lasted for a few minutes."

"And you figure that this is the same thing done on a planetary scale?"  Dutch looks at me waiting for me to tell her how nuts she sounds.  Instead, I sit at my station and start pulling up as much data on the battle as I can.  If Dutch is right then the answer to this problem lies in the past, but I have to move quickly, Mark Ellis, Mouse, and Co can hardly stop a whole planet from finding and killing our people.  Somehow I have to cure my squad and then figure out a way to get everyone below even Mr. Horse Poop Boots on board the Mohawk.

I head down to the Med-pit to find  Sarge and Yeldon stretching after having slept on the floor. Yeldon looks down at herself goes beat red and says "what in the world am I wearing!"

Sarge gets up looks me straight in the eye and says quietly "report."  I tell them both all that has happened including our intelligence buddies down below.  Sarge takes it all in then says, "Yaz I'm keeping you in command.  I'm still muddled and you understand the situation I don't."  I'm crestfallen at that, Sarge seems so normal I was kinda hoping to get back to my minding my own business job and ordering Yeldon to change her socks.  I nod slightly and look over at Yeldon who's playing cat's cradle with a piece of tubing from the medical locker.  I guess the effects aren't a hundred percent off yet.

Yeldon sees me looking at her and then snaps at me "stop looking!  You just want to see me naked again."

Shaking my head I walk out and head back to the bridge to find Dutch gone.  I ask HARVE he tells me she's down with the rocket.  I sit down on the bridge and start to think, the solar flare we passed through was no flare.  It was the edge of the effect.  We're close to where we passed through the flare right now.  Sarge comes in quietly and starts to read the screen.  "I have one big problem right now, how to land something big enough to pull everyone off that planet," I say hoping Sean has regained his brilliance.

"No corporal you have the problem of saving this planet," I twist around thinking the Andi weapon must be effecting Sarge still.

Unfortunately, it isn't.  He points at the readings from the biomonitors and I realize why everyone on the planet is acting the way they are.

"Awwww, this isn't fair," I say.  I look over the readings a second time and they only get worse.  "Every living thing on the planet is degrading.  A slow death by inches.  Literally, they are losing their lives one cell at a time."  My brow grows slick with sweat.  Saving people one at a time with my rifle is more my bag, saving them by the planet load is Sarge's.  I look up hoping he can take over.  He sees the look and reads my thoughts.

He shakes his head, "I still want to go and play hopscotch."

"Hopscotch sounds like a great idea..." I say distracted as Sarge puts me on a whole new track of thought.  Then I glance over some of the reports from the battle with Andi's and how some of the engineers cracked the new weapon problem, and I give a big smile.

"You know how to solve this?"  Sarge asks giving me the eye.

"I do now...thanks Sarge," I say and march off the bridge.

# VIII

Mary looks over the horizon from the top of the rock outcrop, she can't be seen from here not even if someone was right below her.  She breaks out the power optical binoculars, one of the few modern items she has that still works.  Probably because they don't have a computer driving the system, she suspects.  Looking west she sees the mob.  "Still coming this way.  Slowly but they'll get here before sundown.  That witch doctor or whatever he is leading the band.  A wagon with a..." Mary breaks off.

Chandler waits but when he gets no reply he says "a wagon?"

"With a portable gallows," Mary says and lowers the binocs.  Putting them to her eyes one more time she sees the Witch Hunter break the mob into small groups sending them this way and that to broaden the search.  His two big henchmen follow close behind him as he moves forward.

"C'mon down," Chandler suggests but Mary keeps watching.  "They'll get here Mary somehow." After half an hour the leading edge of the mob is at the foot of the hill containing their hideout.

They both hear the booming voice of the Witch Hunter "come down!  We know you are here!"

Chandler and Mary look around the hill, the mob has surrounded it and is starting to move up the slope.  Angry shouts start to fill the air and hearty chuckles in response to jokes made about what will happen to the witches when caught.  Finally, there is nowhere left to run and Mary and Chandler stand at the front of the cave waiting.  The crowd surrounds them and starts to giggle as the wagon is driven around.

Lord Taylon aka Mark Ellis marches out to stand just in front of the mob holding his hands up he says "wait! These two must be sent to Timber for torture and questioning."

One of the villagers fires back, "the hell you say, Hunter.  All you've done is protect the witches and lost two!  These two die now."  With that, the crowd closes in and then stops almost as suddenly as they start.  A hum begins to surround them all. Looking into the sky they see a bright point of light pierce the dirty grayish yellow sky.  The light grows brighter with each passing second until a strange shape resolves out of the glare.  Within only a few seconds a strange apparition hangs ominously above all their heads and then touches the earth lightly landing just in front of the cultural team and

Mark Ellis.  The crowd backs away in fear and some of the quicker thinking start to run back down the hill.

For a moment after the thing stops its engines.  And for a moment, there is a strange quiet.  All even those who started to run stop and watch the tube on stilts.  A seam opens from its middle and a door opens.  Light pours out of the strange object and then a figure much like a man walks out and down the ramp to place booted feet on the ground.

"Stop!"  It says, sounding remarkably male.  As if he has cast a spell the figure gains everyone's attention.  "My name is Corporal Yaz of the United Earth Space Service.  I have come among you to bring knowledge and peace."

# End

That last bit I got from an old movie. The village folk stop and look up at me and wait for my knowledge and peace. I hope it's enough. "I am a man just like you. I am not a witch, I use no magic. This is a machine." I say pointing to the rocket. "Not long ago you yourselves used such machines. But one day they stopped working."

An old woman elbows her way to the head of the crowd looks me up and down and says "you're a StarSoldier ain't ya?"

I breathe out at that, this just got a whole lot easier, "yes I am. You folks are from Earth just like me."

"I remember Earth," a young woman says her eyes mist over with memory. "I remember talking to my parents. But that must be untrue I mean look at this place. All that must be a lie."

I looked down at the woman and smile gently "are you dreaming now? Look at me, look at the machine. All of it is real. Does anyone here remember the Andi wars?" A few people stick their mitts up. I'm amazed that so many admit they do, considering the death penalty for anyone who believes what I'm saying is true. "At some point in the last forty years or so the Andi's released a vapor into the atmosphere, it renders machines useless and over time kills all life forms. The people you call witches work for United Earth and have been trying to figure out what happened here."

Mark Ellis walks around the capsule and looks at me, "corporal you mean what happened here is an Andi weapon?"

"Was agent, was. The test on this planet was done before the battle of Trianglulea. The Andi's were driven out of this area at that battle. If we had lost that space battle, every colony in this sector would have suffered the same fate." I hear the crowd go hush as they realize the Witch Hunter is a witch, and that their long nightmare was caused by a hostile alien race. Worse one they've been denying for years existed.

"Must we remain like this forever or until we die?" Someone in the crowd asks me in a small voice. Hundreds of pairs of eyes look up at me waiting for me to pronounce their fate.

Instead of answering I walk back into the ship and come back out with the contraption Dutch and I knocked together before we landed. With as much confidence as I can muster I show the device to everyone.  "I can and I will reverse the effect.  It will take about ten days for the whole planet to be cleaned of the vapor.  But it will be cleaned."

Mouse comes around and looks up at me, "that's no good Yaz, the Dadus will find out what's going on and stop it.  He has armies.  Someone here will betray us."

I look out over the crowd many have their eyes cast down to the ground, no doubt what Mouse says is true.  As far as it goes.  I give my biggest smile "no Mouse they won't."  I set the machine on the ground about a yard away from the rocket and flip a single silver switch on the side of its body.  The internals start to hum and the lights begin to glow steadily, the crowd watches now fascinated instead of frightened.  With all the bravado I am wont to display at times I take the red key from around my neck place it in the slot and give one twist, and the whole crowd even the United Earth folks including Mouse gasp in delight.  It's as if a rainbow has been exploded into gem-shaped shards that spin and circle the machine in ever increasing orbits.  Some people start to duck and I hold up my hand "let the light penetrate you, please.  It's curing the damage to your bodies, it will not harm you."

The old woman smiles at the display and says finally "Aw hell why not?  All I can do is die sooner."  And with that, she stands tall spreading her hands out and letting the light dance around her.  Soon the air around us clears the muddy smog breaks up and starts to dissipate as the rainbow of light keeps flying higher and higher into the sky shards seeming to dance on the wind.  We all watch as a tunnel is drilled through the murk and all at once we see the topaz of the sky that earned this world its name.  And with it, the area around us is flooded in sunlight, rich, warm yellow sunlight and everyone starts to laugh and clap their hands.

Mark Ellis puts his hand on my shoulder, "how did you figure it out?"

"I didn't Dutch did, she fought at Triangulea and remembered the weapon.  After that, we started to decipher the strange radiation signatures and came up with this."  I say pointing my toe at the machine.

Ellis gives me a mischievous grin saying "lucky I only kicked you around huh?" He gives my shoulder a squeeze, "who says StarSoldier are just dumb gun-toting jocks?  Mouse is right nonetheless, the Dadus is coming his power is based on the world staying the way it is.  Ten days will take too long.  I can guarantee you there is a spy here."

"How long will it take for him to get here?"

"Not long, a week," Ellis says.

"By then my squad will be sorted out and ready, more to the point so will these people.  The Dadus is about to find the world very changed.  I'm willing to bet that as the sun shines through the gloom people will give up on the Dadus."

"Most, not all," Mark says.  I nod.  I know he's right.  Once people get an idea in their head it takes a lot to shift it.  But if most people in the colony change their point of view the Dadus is done.

# Feedback

---

Please leave honest feedback.
Your opinion is important to me!

# Beta Readers Wanted

# My Email

---

cr.coyne@yahoo.com

*Looking forward to hearing from you!  Please email your desire to be a beta reader.*

# Who I am

I love telling stories and the more out of this world the better.  I hope you enjoy my musings as much as I enjoy spinning them.  I spend my time writing, running my business, riding my bike too fast everywhere and catering to my cat Ares! Oh, and writing.

# COPYRIGHT

---

© copyright C.R. Coyne 2024

# Prisoners

A StarSoldier Chronicle

C.R. Coyne

"The night is long that never finds the day."—
William Shakespeare: McBeth

"I don't mind telling you I'm scared." She says in hushed tones though the lab is completely soundproof. He looks over at her no expression on his face as he works the strange arrangement of devices in front of him. "I suppose that doesn't mean much to you, having no emotions."

His mouth twists at the jab proving under the cold exterior exists some emotion just buried deep enough he could control it, most of the time. He puts down the alien instrument and turns to face her, for the first time that evening. "I also have qualms about this project regardless of what you may think of my emotional state. But I believe we and I do me we Doctor Xu will make history tonight. I believe there is a purpose in all things, even if we don't immediately see it. You and I finding this place, all this technology from a lost civilization, that must mean something.  Shall we begin?"

She looks at his excitement and the desire in his eyes and smiles gently, "why not?  History waits for no man, or so I am told."

"You know if this works we'll be able to find out if that is true."  He moves the toggle to the right and the small telltale lights up green and the flow of power begins.  The subtle glow of the alien device was expected and both scientists smile as their predictions are proven true.  While watching they begin to hear the worrying sound of the generator starting to spin faster and faster.  That was not supposed to happen. "Shut it off!"  Doctor Xu screams as the light from the device becomes unbearable the generator now howling as it tries to give what the device demands.  He races around the table toward the generator only to stop, the heat coming from the device is incredible, how it's still functioning is unbelievable.  Still, the alien contraption purrs getting brighter, starting to make its own high pitched whistle tearing at their ears until they bleed.  "Jonathon!"  She screams as the expected gateway opens, she sees the strange shadow begin to emerge from the device.  At first, it looked for all the world human.  But as extra legs and a tail begin to show it transforms into a nightmare.  One claw reaches out to touch a new land.  Like a man testing the temperature of water, the thing slowly slips past the energy curtain that separates it from its world into ours.  Doctor Xu pushes away her chair and races behind to find Jonathon lying dead on the floor burned to a crisp. She knows it's her death to go on, but scientist that she is, she knows her duty in a failed experiment and pushes past the heat and shimmering energy and yanks the wire shrieking in agony as the alien energy tears at her body burning the flesh from her face and hands.

As the power is cut the thing comes through hefting a strange crystalline hand weapon.  It stands there watching the death of the bi-ped.  It tests the gravity of this new place rising and falling on all six legs smiles and takes a deep breath of the strange chemical mix, it's foul but breathable.  The bi-ped casts one eye on it then exhales and lies limp.  It was always so with the first ones.  Those that would presume to learn the secrets of the Hota.  It walks calmly and snaps the wires back in, after all, what was the use of being alone in a new land?